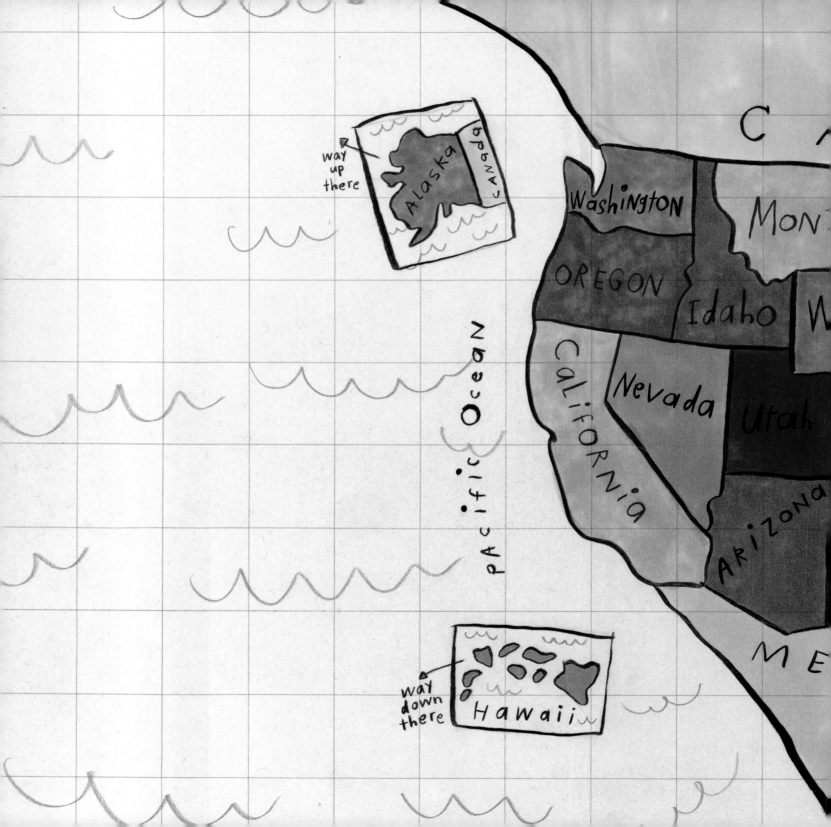

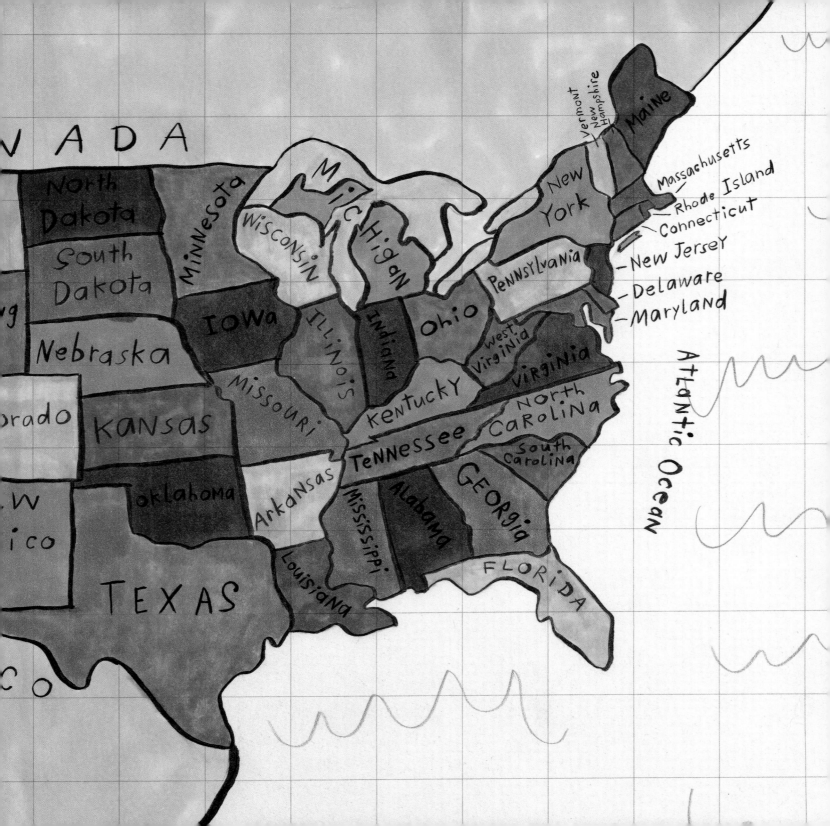

This book is dedicated to my mom.
I love you.
–Laurie

THIS BOOK BELONGS TO:
_____

WHO LIVES IN THE STATE OF:
_____

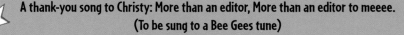
A thank-you song to Christy: More than an editor, More than an editor to meeee.
(To be sung to a Bee Gees tune)

ISBN 0-439-13346-7

Copyright © 1998 by Laurie Keller. All rights reserved.
Published by Scholastic Inc., 555 Broadway, New York, NY 10012,
by arrangement with Henry Holt and Company, Inc. SCHOLASTIC
and associated logos are trademarks and/or
registered trademarks of Scholastic Inc.

12 11 10 9 8 7 6 5 4 3 2 1                    9/9 0 1 2 3 4/0

Printed in the U.S.A.                    08

First Scholastic printing, September 1999

The artist used acrylic paint, colored pencils, marker, and collage
on illustration board to create the illustrations for this book.
Factual information about the states on pages 32 to 35 is from
*The Doubleday Atlas of the United States of America*,
by Josephine Bacon (New York: Doubleday, 1990).

# the SCRAMBLED STATES of AMERICA

By LAURIE KELLER

**SCHOLASTIC INC.**
New York   Toronto   London   Auckland   Sydney
Mexico City   New Delhi   Hong Kong

# HI THERE.

I'm Sam. I'm assuming since you opened this book that you're in the mood to hear a story. Well, you're in luck, because I have a story for you. It's a little story about this fine country of ours. I'll bet you thought you'd heard 'em all, but not many people know this one.

Hi, I'M New Jersey. I'M NOT new and I'm not wearing a Jersey. Go Figure!

Do You MiNd?!

Idaho

Hi. I'm a staR. A star with a hat.

Let ME tell it!

Oh, oh, let ME! Let ME!

**No,** no, you two— that part is my job. Now get back in your places. We're about to start the story.

Aren't they cute?

Let's give them a couple of seconds to get back into position. One thousand ONE. One thousand TWO. One thousand THREE.

## OK, turn the page!

*! ⊙ #
I could've ⊚
told it!…

Well, it was just your basic, ordinary day in the good old U.S. of A. States all over the country were waking up, having their first cups of coffee, reading the morning paper, and enjoying the beautiful sunrise.

↑ (Up there a ways –
connected to Canada)

ALASKA

CANADA

(the largest state in the U.S.A.)

WASHINGTON

MONTANA

MINNESOTA

NORTH DAKOTA

Time to
get up.

PACIFIC OCEAN

OREGON

IDAHO

SOUTH DAKOTA

IOWA

WYOMING

ZZZ

NEBRASKA

MISSOURI

NEVADA

CALIFORNIA

UTAH

COLORADO

KANSAS

OKLAHOMA

ARIZONA

TEXAS

NEW MEXICO

Good
morning.

Good
morning.

MEXICO

Hi

HAWAII

Wake up
sleepy heads.

↓ ( Down there a ways – 2,100 miles
southwest of California)

All the states, that is,
**except for Kansas.**

He was not feeling happy at all.

**How do I know this?**
Because he said,

I'M NOT FEELING HAPPY AT ALL!

Close-up of KANSAS

SUNFLOWER

(State flower of Kansas)

NEBRASKA

KANSAS

**"What's wrong?"**
his best friend, Nebraska, kindly asked him.
(Nebraska is a very kind state.)

WANT AN ACORN?
I LOVE 'EM!

"I don't know," moaned Kansas. "I just feel bored. All day long we just sit here in the middle of the country. We never **GO** anywhere. We never **DO** anything, and we **NEVER** meet any **NEW** states!"

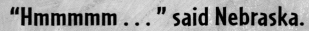

"Hmmmmm . . ." said Nebraska.

"Don't get me wrong, Nebraska. You're the best friend a state could have.

But don't you ever want more? Don't you ever want to see what else is out there?"

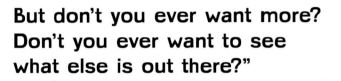

Nebraska's thought process →

"Yes! Yes, I do!" Nebraska said excitedly. "And now that you mention it, I'm sick and tired of hearing North Dakota and South Dakota bicker all the time!"

Me, too!

# I HAVE A GREAT IDEA!

exclaimed Kansas.

(WOW! His smile is 285 miles wide!)

Kansas
Scale of Miles
0 10 20 30 40 50

"Let's have a party and invite all the other states!
You know, one of those get-to-know-you deals.
Everyone can bring a favorite dish. We could have
music and dancing. . . ."

"That's a GREAT idea!"
shrieked Nebraska.
"I wish I'd thought of it myself."

So, with a little help from their neighbors, Missouri and Iowa,
those wacky little midwestern states planned the biggest party ever.

They sent out invitations,

and blew up balloons.

They even hired a band to play.

At last, the big day came, and little by little the states arrived at the party. Nebraska and Kansas were on the welcoming committee, Iowa was in charge of coats, and Missouri and Illinois passed out name tags for each state to wear.

WOW! Those Southwestern states can really dance!

CALIFORNIA Fruit Salad

IOWA CORN SURPRISE

IDAHO

Minnesota

TEXAS

Montana

Ohio

Allow me.

Thank you.

Wyoming

This is the third time I've dropped my fork!

Have you tried the Alabama peanut bars?

Within minutes after their arrival, the states began making friends with each other. They spent hours talking, laughing, dancing, and singing.

It was long into the evening when Idaho and Virginia got up on the stage.

"Excuse me," Idaho said politely. (Idaho is a very polite state.) "Sorry to interrupt, but Virginia and I were just talking and we thought it might be fun if she and I switched places—you know—so we could see a new part of the country."

"Yes," Virginia chimed in. "Then we thought maybe all of you might want to try it, too. What do you think?"

Hello, my name is: VIRGINIA

Hello, my name is: IDAHO

LORADO

NEW M

FLORIDA

CALIFORNIA

**A wave of excitement swept through the room.**

**They could hardly wait.**
**Immediately, the states made their plans to switch places.**
**They said their good-byes, and went directly home to pack.**

It took the better part of the next morning for the states to move to their new spots, but finally they were settled in. All of the states were much happier now that they were by their new neighbors and in a new part of the country. Oh yes, this was a much better arrangement!

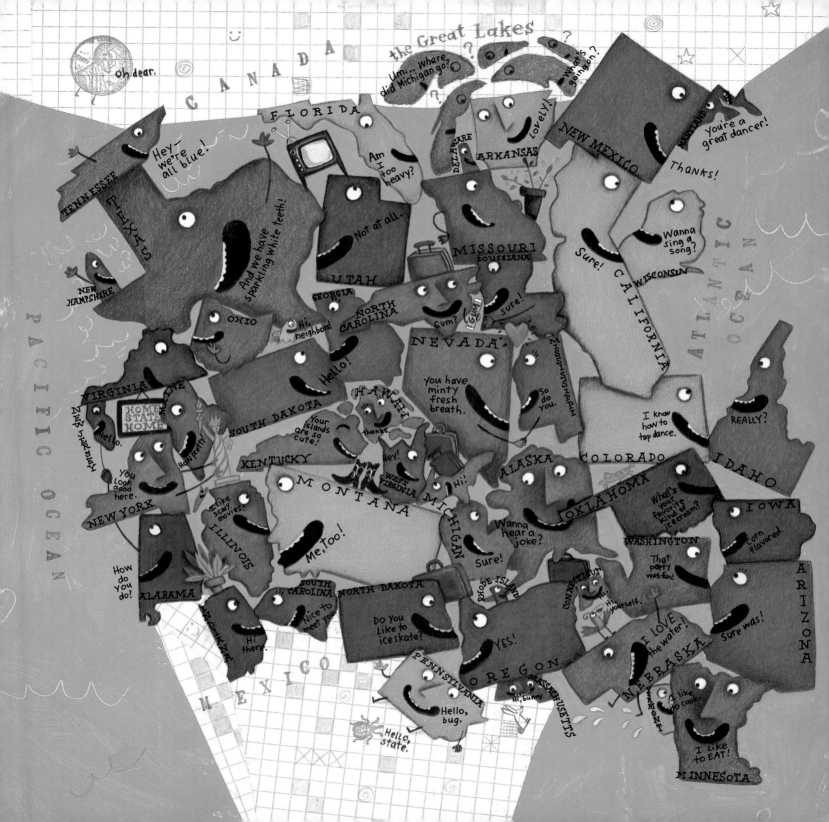

**But after a couple of days had passed and all the excitement had died down, the states began to realize that they weren't as happy as they thought.**

Florida, who had switched spots with Minnesota, was FREEZING in the frosty northern climate. And Minnesota, who forgot to buy sunscreen, got an awful sunburn.

FLORiDA

BBBRRRR!

Hutchooo! TEXAS

Thanks, pal!

A BIG HUG will make your SUNBURN feel better!

MiNNeSoTA

VT.

YYYOOUUUCH!

NeBRaska

NEW YORK

ALABAMA

Oh, No!

INDIANA

Alabama, New York, and Indiana—all of whom took California's place—were bothered by an annoying rumbling sound that kept them up all night.

Want some CHEESE?

WiSCONSiN

Eeeooo! Get it away! I'M Lactose intolerant!

CaLiFORNiA

Well, Excuse me!

Arizona, who had traded places with South Carolina, was upset because the ocean waves kept ruining her hairdo.

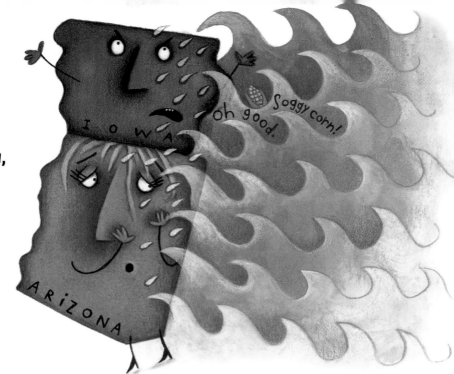

Alaska, who had been wanting a little more interaction with the other states, was irritated by Oklahoma's handle jabbing into his left side and Michigan's thumb tickling his right.

**And worst of all,** Kansas, who had switched places with Hawaii
because he was sick of being stuck in the middle of the country,
was now stuck in the middle of NOWHERE, feeling lonesome and seasick.

IN THE MIDDLE OF NOWHERE
FEELIN' LONESOME AND SEASICK,

KANSAS

MY GUITAR IS SOGGY
AND I FEEL SO BLUE...

It's
so
sad.

R.I.P.

(And Hawaii was longing for some peace and quiet like in the good old days.)

Well, there was no question in any state's mind about what to do. Everyone wanted to go home! So, even faster than they made the first trip, they packed up their things and hit the road.

Yes, my name is Illinois and I need one airline ticket to...um...Well, Illinois... mmmhmmm... no, the "S" is silent.

Want a ride?

Sure!

Do you have any 3's?

GO FISH!

BUS STOP

As the sun set across the country, all of the states–from A to W– were back in their very own homes. The states were so happy to see their old friends again. They spent the entire evening sharing their new experiences with each other– the good and the bad.

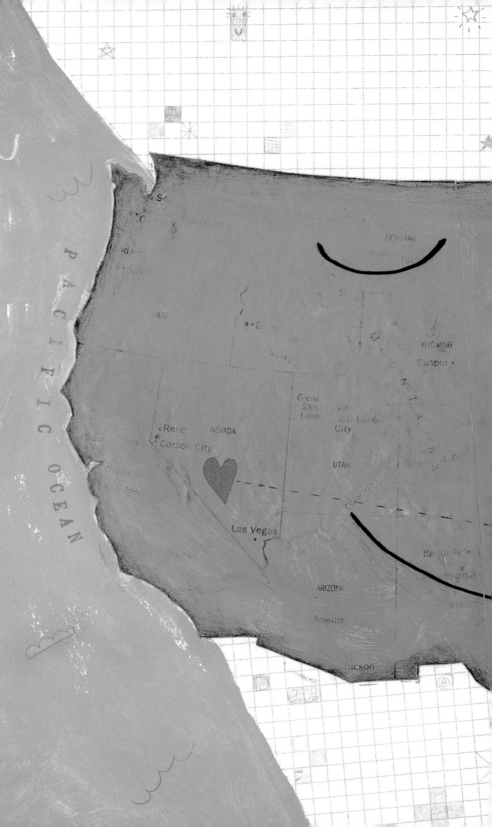

That night, all the states in the country went to bed feeling happy about the new friends they had made but, most of all, feeling very thankful to be home.

"Heart of Dixie"
ALABAMA
Capital: Montgomery
Square Miles: 50,767
Population: 4,083,000

"The Last Frontier"
ALASKA
Capital: Juneau
Square Miles: 570,830
Population: 525,000

"Grand Canyon State"
ARIZONA
Capital: Phoenix
Square Miles: 113,508
Population: 3,386,000

"Land of Opportunity"
ARKANSAS
Capital: Little Rock
Square Miles: 52,078
Population: 2,388,000

"Golden State"
CALIFORNIA
Capital: Sacramento
Square Miles: 156,299
Population: 27,663,000

"Centennial State"
COLORADO
Capital: Denver
Square Miles: 103,595
Population: 3,296,000

"Constitution State"
CONNECTICUT
Capital: Hartford
Square Miles: 4,872
Population: 3,211,000

"First State"
DELAWARE
Capital: Dover
Square Miles: 1,932
Population: 644,000

"Sunshine State"
FLORIDA
Capital: Tallahassee
Square Miles: 54,153
Population: 12,023,000

"Empire State of the South"
GEORGIA
Capital: Atlanta
Square Miles: 58,056
Population: 6,222,000

"Aloha State"
HAWAII
Capital: Honolulu
Square Miles: 6,425
Population: 1,083,000

"Gem State"
IDAHO
Capital: Boise
Square Miles: 82,412
Population: 998,000

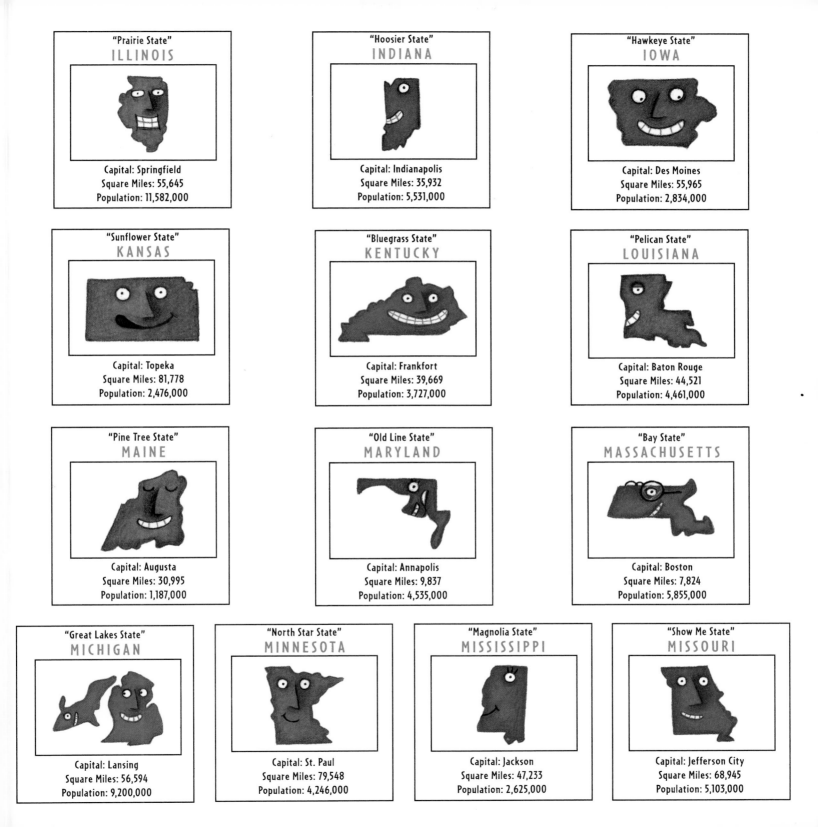

**"Prairie State"**
## ILLINOIS
Capital: Springfield
Square Miles: 55,645
Population: 11,582,000

**"Hoosier State"**
## INDIANA
Capital: Indianapolis
Square Miles: 35,932
Population: 5,531,000

**"Hawkeye State"**
## IOWA
Capital: Des Moines
Square Miles: 55,965
Population: 2,834,000

**"Sunflower State"**
## KANSAS
Capital: Topeka
Square Miles: 81,778
Population: 2,476,000

**"Bluegrass State"**
## KENTUCKY
Capital: Frankfort
Square Miles: 39,669
Population: 3,727,000

**"Pelican State"**
## LOUISIANA
Capital: Baton Rouge
Square Miles: 44,521
Population: 4,461,000

**"Pine Tree State"**
## MAINE
Capital: Augusta
Square Miles: 30,995
Population: 1,187,000

**"Old Line State"**
## MARYLAND
Capital: Annapolis
Square Miles: 9,837
Population: 4,535,000

**"Bay State"**
## MASSACHUSETTS
Capital: Boston
Square Miles: 7,824
Population: 5,855,000

**"Great Lakes State"**
## MICHIGAN
Capital: Lansing
Square Miles: 56,594
Population: 9,200,000

**"North Star State"**
## MINNESOTA
Capital: St. Paul
Square Miles: 79,548
Population: 4,246,000

**"Magnolia State"**
## MISSISSIPPI
Capital: Jackson
Square Miles: 47,233
Population: 2,625,000

**"Show Me State"**
## MISSOURI
Capital: Jefferson City
Square Miles: 68,945
Population: 5,103,000

"Treasure State"
MONTANA
Capital: Helena
Square Miles: 145,388
Population: 809,000

"Cornhusker State"
NEBRASKA
Capital: Lincoln
Square Miles: 76,644
Population: 1,594,000

"Sagebrush State"
NEVADA
Capital: Carson City
Square Miles: 109,894
Population: 1,007,000

"Granite State"
NEW HAMPSHIRE
Capital: Concord
Square Miles: 8,993
Population: 1,057,000

"Garden State"
NEW JERSEY
Capital: Trenton
Square Miles: 7,468
Population: 7,672,000

"Land of Enchantment"
NEW MEXICO
Capital: Santa Fe
Square Miles: 121,335
Population: 1,500,000

"Empire State"
NEW YORK
Capital: Albany
Square Miles: 47,377
Population: 17,825,000

"Tar Heel State"
NORTH CAROLINA
Capital: Raleigh
Square Miles: 48,843
Population: 6,413,000

"Peace Garden State"
NORTH DAKOTA
Capital: Bismarck
Square Miles: 69,300
Population: 672,000

"Buckeye State"
OHIO
Capital: Columbus
Square Miles: 41,004
Population: 10,784,000

"Sooner State"
OKLAHOMA
Capital: Oklahoma City
Square Miles: 68,655
Population: 3,272,000

"Beaver State"
OREGON
Capital: Salem
Square Miles: 96,184
Population: 2,724,000

"Keystone State"
**PENNSYLVANIA**
Capital: Harrisburg
Square Miles: 44,888
Population: 11,936,000

"Ocean State"
**RHODE ISLAND**
Capital: Providence
Square Miles: 1,055
Population: 947,154

"Palmetto State"
**SOUTH CAROLINA**
Capital: Columbia
Square Miles: 30,203
Population: 3,425,000

"Coyote State"
**SOUTH DAKOTA**
Capital: Pierre
Square Miles: 75,952
Population: 709,000

"Volunteer State"
**TENNESSEE**
Capital: Nashville
Square Miles: 41,155
Population: 4,855,000

"Lone Star State"
**TEXAS**
Capital: Austin
Square Miles: 262,017
Population: 16,789,000

"Beehive State"
**UTAH**
Capital: Salt Lake City
Square Miles: 82,073
Population: 1,680,000

"Green Mountain State"
**VERMONT**
Capital: Montpelier
Square Miles: 9,273
Population: 548,000

"Old Dominion"
**VIRGINIA**
Capital: Richmond
Square Miles: 39,704
Population: 5,904,000

"Evergreen State"
**WASHINGTON**
Capital: Olympia
Square Miles: 66,511
Population: 4,409,000

"Mountain State"
**WEST VIRGINIA**
Capital: Charleston
Square Miles: 24, 119
Population: 1,897,000

"Badger State"
**WISCONSIN**
Capital: Madison
Square Miles: 54,426
Population: 4,807,000

"Equality State"
**WYOMING**
Capital: Cheyenne
Square Miles: 96,989
Population: 509,000

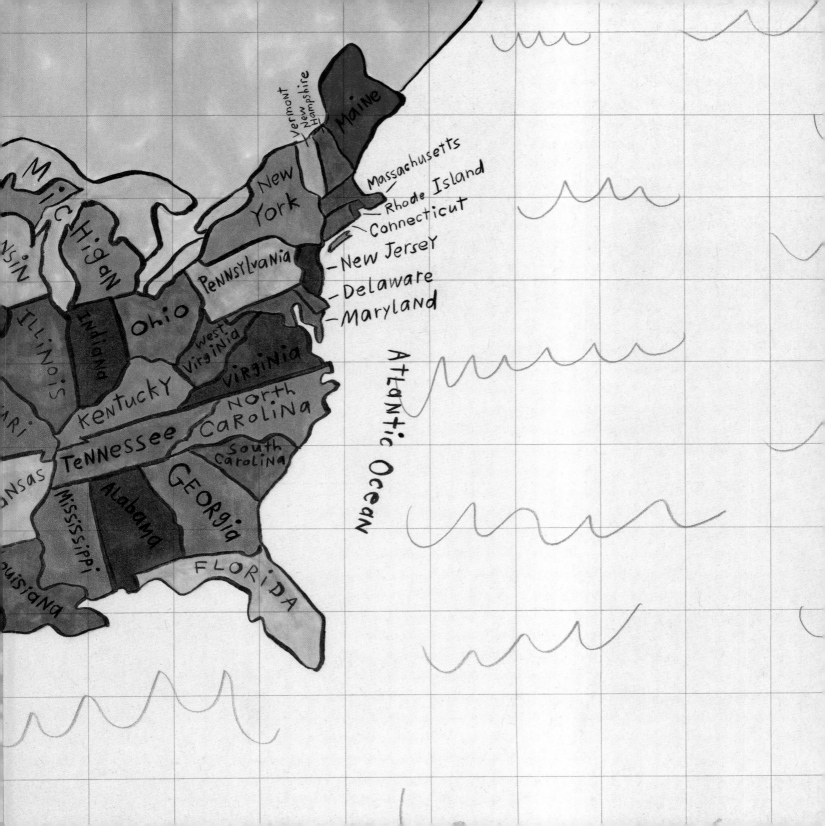